RATTLE IN THE HEAD

PALMETTO
PUBLISHING
Charleston, SC
www.PalmettoPublishing.com

Copyright © 2024 by Darth Nuada

All rights reserved
No portion of this book may be reproduced, stored in a retrieval system, or transmitted in any form by any means–electronic, mechanical, photocopy, recording, or other–except for brief quotations in printed reviews, without prior permission of the author.

Paperback: ISBN 9798822959262
eBook ISBN: 9798822959279

DARTH NUADA
RATTLE IN THE HEAD

CHAPTER 1

My name is G., and although I dread telling it, this is my story. I don't put ink to paper on this subject lightly. It could make my life much worse, could make me loved, but will likely make me hated. However, my community, tribe, and even nation, which I hate, are more important than myself. I didn't always despise America; I used to be a patriot among patriots. Even served in the military at a time, but what they have done to me has driven me to destroy them. Due to their own nature, it will be more efficient to start their destruction with the pen and end it with the rifle. My enemy is very well armed, extremely capable, and hideously covetous. Thankfully, the depth of their evil deeds is so appalling that once the majority of the population knows of them, their time tormenting us will be drastically reduced. It should be known that I hate the government of the United States, not the people. I am no longer racist like I was in high school. That said, I understand racism and why it exists in about every person I've met and all branches of the government. It is a foundational cinder block of humanity at its most tribalistic level.

As a child I grew up all over the western United States. My family and roots are from an Indian Reservation in California. For the first four years we were on the reservation. My father worked in the forest service and when I was four, we moved to a remote part of Oregon just north of Prospect. We lived in forest service housing. I vividly remember it being a stunningly beautiful dense forest with so many deer you had to stop to let the herds cross the road. Not in Prospect though people help themselves to the deer when they can that far out. We used to fish in a canoe on the mighty Rogue River. Oregon was a very free place, far from the police state it is today. I imagine my grandfather could remember when California was the same way. I remember my gramps and a relative named bund. Who was in the backseat but was too fat to put the seatbelt on. Bund said ('It's too small, I can't get it around my stomach.') Gramps said ('just use a rope.') Our neighbor Jim with his long graying beard lent my dad a copy of *Halo CE*, my brother and I's favorite game at the time on Xbox. Before we played it, I had this reoccurring terrifying dream. I was in a room and three invisible figures wearing kill hats, surrounded me towering over me. At the time I had no idea what a kill hat was. They would never make a sound. I felt as if they telekinetically inserted an indominable amount of fear and utter terror in me. I had this dream three times in my life and finally understand it.

I was a curious child always exploring my dad, being the expert woodsman he was, bought a walker hound. Dad said, ('Hounds are very loyal they'll fight to the death to protect their family, especially kids.') Dad knew Western Oregon was home to some of the biggest mountain lions in North America.

Trusty sat between my brother and I on our way back from Medford. My first friend besides my brother was Jacob. We went to pre-school and kindergarten together, racing to put our winter gear on to go outside and use the snow-covered playground. I remember getting my first tetanus shot. Which I hated lol, disturbingly I remember my brother having some growth removed from his arm. When he came out of the room in agony I smiled, and my mom asked why I did it. I didn't know why; I would kill to protect my brother. I felt some odd and terribly powerful presence while smiling, as well as shame and disgust for doing so. In 2007 we moved back to the rez.

My brother and I would fish and run around our family land assignment. Both my dad's piece and my uncle's; sometimes we got along back then. Our family has had the land since the reservation was founded. There is a rumor about my family that some people on the rez believe. It goes like this; the original Native man who lived here was named Fred. He lived in a house with his wife Alanya. Fred worked his ass off; he was a selfless man but too kind for his own good. His wife was a slut she got with an outsider named Mar, a black man whose grandad was a freedman who came west. The rumor is that Mar murdered Fred, then took his wife and house. The truth is when Alanya cheated on Fred, he couldn't or as I believe just didn't kick her out. Fred was the man who kept the fences up and made sure my grandmother's kids had firewood. He never refrigerated his food. The cheese would be green sometimes. ('It was alright we just cut the green parts out, dad said.') Fred was very depressed, used to go on weeklong drunks. During these he would go into his old house with his old wife and say ('This is my house').

Before he was kicked out, Fred had a daughter we'll call Freyja, she is my grandmother. Freyja had three more siblings Mer, Son, and Cook. Fred still sweated and followed the old ways of praying. Freyja is Fred's only biological heir. Mar did not kill Fred, and my dad said ('He was a good man.')

Fred used to shoot deer with a .22. He would shoot them in the head, preferably in the ear from the side. Once they were home, he'd string them up in the old oak near Gram's house and make jerky out of them. They would also boil deer because they didn't have money to buy lard. Without running water, Freyja would carry water from the river to the house. If Fred shot a very large deer, he would carry it back in halves. He got one this big near Mule Peak, that's the only one I was told about but I know there were others. At times it was rough. Freyja used to walk to school, just a few miles, but she said ('I got to school one day so exhausted I passed out and when I got up, a teacher gave me some juice to keep me awake until lunch.')

Gram spoke about her friend Lenny bringing over bread sometimes. She looked at bread like it was a cookie. Freyja had Jones, Bu, Jolly, Orange, and Chunk. She had these kids with a white man of Livonian decent, we'll call him Wick. Freyja fucked Bear man while she had her kids in the bed next to her, including my dad Jones. From that day forward, this family has been fucked up. This man's nickname was Bear, so I'll call him that in this story. Wick was falling timber at the time. A man named Calvin, Bear's friend, was taunting him. ('I heard Bear was fucking Freyja.') Wick started fighting him, and while wrestling Calvin grabbed a 45 automatic off the wooden table near them. Wick's words were ('I saw that .45 one time then I turned it around and the gun fired.) Calvin fell backward into the tent. There had to be witnesses because there was an Indian fire crew there.

This was significant because outsiders had been killed for far less then killing an Indian here. However, it was understood Calvin had it coming. This burden stayed on Wick's mind for the rest of his days. This family was dysfunctional. The eldest got everything and the younger children just got anything that was left, or a much cheaper version of what the eldest got. My dad was treated like shit. His brother Bu shot him with a pellet gun close enough to stick in his flesh. Later he shot my dad from about sixty-five yards away with a 12-gauge. Dad had a .22 and wanted to return fire, but as he said, ('I was worried he would blind me with the bird shot').

I moved back home to live around my family just before I turned twenty-one and landed a job. When I was eighteen, I found out what the Patriot Act was and decided to raise hell for the NSA. I got more than what I imagined they were capable of. I decided since they were violating my fellow citizen's rights, I'd try to draw attention to me to distract them from other Americans. In general, a fuck you to them.

Although I did, at the time, sell weed to make most of my money, I exaggerated my business and told my girl all about it. I wasn't aware yet, but my girl Em had been raped. Now, the paranormal shit. That girl was haunted. I was a science-based man at the time, but I didn't actively refuse to accept supernatural things. Most science-based people deny what they see because it does not fit their idea of what the world is. She invited me over, when I got there, we went downstairs to the basement where her room was. It was cozy down there and awesome. We would play *Mortal Kombat* and fuck on the couch. One night I was on top of her, clapping her cheeks way into it. She loved being choked. About thirty minutes in a person peeked at us. From around the door, just the head though. Her bedroom was on the left side of the hallway in the basement. You walked down into the basement, turned right, walked down the hall, and it was the last door on your left.

At the end of the hallway was the bathroom. The man wasn't flesh and blood though, just a shadow version of a man's head. I could see eyebrows but no other facial features. I was enjoying watching her face contort in pleasure LMFAO I was having too much fun to stop; her pussy was so tight. A few weeks later she came to me in her cute little outfit. She looked good, fresh from the big city. ('G… will you help me? I get choked by a red eyed man every time I go to sleep.') She lived in a very nice upper middle class white neighborhood, which made me believe her when she said her parents didn't believe her. I let her know I would help where I can. I asked if she watches horror films. She didn't, no horror books, not even horror video games. Fuck, I thought… have you ever done anything that could have stuck something with you? Her response ('When I was seven my friends and I played Bloody Mary in the bathroom next to my room. We got scared and never closed the game.')

I thought to myself, ('Shit, she might be haunted.') I doubted it would even matter if she did close the game; playing it would be enough. It sure seemed like it. I thought let's fuck this ghost up. I told her to research how to get rid of an evil spirit. I didn't have sage. She decided to bind it into a Bible. At first, I said we'll tell it to leave but her heart wasn't in it 100 percent. I can still remember how the room felt, as if there was an apex predator looking at us just behind the walls. The binding worked. Everything was awesome.

I got a job doing foundation work and she was a barista. Curiosity killed the cat; I opened up the book, which broke the seal of wax. Things quickly went downhill; we broke up in three weeks. By the end of September, she met up with me just to threaten to kill our baby out of spite. I didn't know she was pregnant, and it made my chest sink, but I held it together. When I got home, I ran three miles and wept like a defeated idiot. Thankfully it turned out to just be a lie she crafted to cause me pain. I gave her the things she had at my place and blocked her. I didn't have any intention of dealing with her anymore.

Directly after all of that, my dad turned back into a complete prick, like he was when I was a kid. My siblings and I used to love summer because he would be gone on fire assignments. He is the best man I have ever met. However, in the late 2000s he fractured three disks in his back. There were mornings where he couldn't move, and I would have to bring him an empty Aluminum Coors bottle to pee in. The only thing the Federal Government did was try to fire my dad. If they succeeded, then they didn't have to pay for his retirement because he still needed one year. At this time my dad was really fucking mean.

My mother refused to get a job because she wanted us to move back to the reservation. She was always doing anything her mom told her even if it put the family through hell. This is why I never date women whose mom's control everything they do. I always got the worst of the beatings because I was the eldest son, and in Dad's childhood it was the eldest who got spoiled. Most weren't terrible, I'm not a bitch. I was introduced to the belt when I was very young lol as every kid should be. This time was different. I was in the shop working on taking off a head gasket or helping at least. I pissed him off. I'm sure I did something, grabbed the wrong wrench or something similar. He hit me on the thumb with the wrench he had, and my hand was on fire, then it went numb. For two weeks my thumb didn't work like it should but healed up. I told my mom, but she ignored it. She was only interested in getting us back to the reservation. Looking back, it was the right thing to do because CPS would have just destroyed our family and laughed at us.

I was not allowed to ever leave the house. When I did hang out with a friend, I came back to find out my dad had been talking shit, saying I never help around there, and I just fucked off all the time. Nothing was ever good enough, my writing, my grades, my anything. We lived in the desert from roughly 2009 to 2013. After that we were on the Reservation until I became a freshman in 2015; that's when we returned to the desert.

Things were different now; my childhood friends were not the same. I attended an extremely prejudiced high school; everyone would salute with a straight arm. Suck Trump in any way possible. I had almost no opinion on politics, but my god, I could play basketball. That was the goal. After school I would do sprints and practice dribbling and shooting. I lived next to an impressive man who was a farmer, and from what I heard, an unbelievably good wrestler. He looked like a white gorilla lol. Mr. C wouldn't care if you ran in his fields even though some druggy assholes would break his sprinklers. Finally, the day came, and I went to tryouts where my fears were proven foolish. I was unstoppable against anyone except the top two varsity guys. I folded my opponents in every drill we ran. I missed one-quarter of my left-handed lay ups, and I was boiling with rage toward myself for not making 100 percent of my shots.

Compared to the competition I was chilling, but that's not how this worked. I wasn't selected, and the friends I made in tryouts (everyone wanted to run team drills with me) didn't believe me. They laughed at me and said, "See you at practice, bro. We're a fucking team!" When they found out it was true, people thought I was confused for T. A half-black dude who was my bro and kind of looked like me. I have more slanted eyes though.

This turned me into a delinquent. Basketball was what kept me a productive student. Without it I was essentially a man who had no reason to regard the rules except to avoid injury or death. I would skip class and never did my homework or gave a fuck about any subject except history and war. Specifically, how to conquer, assimilate, or just outright destroy other cultures and nations. I found one similarity in all the wars I've ever read about. It doesn't matter how much you destroy a nation of people. You can never truly conquer them unless you kill them all or destroy their culture. There are examples of this in abundance if you read about history. Genghis Khan, also known as Temujin, would tell the city he arrived at to surrender. If they did not, he would completely destroy them. Killing everyone inside except the most beautiful women to rape, as well as engineers or people with extremely valuable trades which could serve his empire.

The British Empire killed all the men on a small island off the coast of New Zealand. The bastards made their wives wear the heads of their husbands as necklaces. The English told the Māori what they had done, and that resistance was suicide. However, the Māori were appalled at the colonizer's evil deeds so much that it psychologically worked against them. The Māori showed the savages from Europe no mercy; they killed and ate them. This news terrorized the most disciplined military in the world and ruined morale, which resulted in them getting their asses kicked by a mere remnant of a once-great nation. All this was done after the colonizers gave the locals guns and watched them kill each other. They knew what they were doing. Assuming that after smallpox and the massive loss of life from the introduction of firearms, the Māori would lay down and submit or be small enough in number to completely exterminate. They were geniuses in their plan to conquer that group of people. They fucked up when they mentioned what they did to the other island. Most importantly, they forgot who they were fighting. They believed the propaganda that told them they were fighting godless savages. However, the reality was they were the godless savages and by threatening the Māori with their past deeds they showed the Māori their horns. Being a nation who understood there is truly a higher power, the Māori knew they faced monsters that needed to be slaughtered like the beasts they had chosen to be. They did exactly that. Ecclesiastes 1:9 KJV ('The thing that hath been, it is that which shall be and that which is done: and there is no new thing under the sun.')

Since I wasn't playing sports, I started drinking and when I was sixteen, I got stoned for the first time. It was fucking awesome. Looking at the stars in a desert is something most people will never get to enjoy like I did. At seventeen, we moved to a remote town in the Northwest. My dad got to retire and moved back to the town he lived in while in the forest service we'll call it Lake town. We still had about a month until school started. Since we lived out of town I could just run and explore this awesome new place. While bored I decided to make a bow but broke one of my rules. I got drunk while making it and the first time I fucked up. Putting my hand below my blade, I cut my hand and cut it good. I couldn't get it to stop bleeding, so I went to the hospital, and they sewed me up. I stopped working out and went looking for weed.

When we arrived here, I was slightly panicked. This place was even more white than the desert; this could be very bad. Fortunately, that's not how it was at all, and these were good people. Better people than me lmfao. I was walking to class with my hand in a wrap, terrified... how the fuck am I going to defend myself with just my right? My plan was to lie low and hope I didn't have to fight until my hand was healed. Meanwhile, at school I was in no danger at all, I was good. I even had this beautiful green-eyed woman flirting with me her ass probably weighed one-quarter of her total weight. She was cool as fuck, so I went over to her place and had dinner with her family. We watched one of the original *Star Wars* films, and I slapped her ass when it was just us in the kitchen lmfao, I was a fucking heathen. She loved it. I have been through hell, but I have always been blessed in bed. We met up again, and out of respect for her current man... I'll leave it at that. I had clapped a few chicks before I moved but I liked this girl. After we split, I was sad but hid it well.

A week later I bought a monkey bar, which is a chocolate bar with mushrooms. I heard shrooms would make me face my fears and could help me get rid of sadness or depression. It certainly did cure that... although the first two hours where terrible lol I was in a loop and kept seeing a gymnasium full of people. I tried to make it stop, but once I asked what the issue was it showed me that I needed to respect people more and when I agreed to do so, the last four hours were pure bliss. Weeks later I had the reoccurring nightmare of the three kill hats, but I had no idea what that was at the time. This was the second time it happened. That same night I also had a nightmare where my beautiful brown wife died, and I couldn't stop it from happening. That dream disturbed me more than any other and I never told anyone about it. These things happened before Em and before I broke the seal when I was nineteen.

Back to after me and Em broke up; I couldn't get right, but when I did, I started kicking ass in community college until covid shut it down and I had to say goodbye to my beautiful pawg girlfriend. I was home for a few weeks and while sleeping was attacked. I heard a goat screaming and then something shiveringly cold was over me. I was on fire with rage. I wanted to murder whatever it was but could only move my right hand. I called out to the almighty, ('fight for me like you did for David and his people.') Whatever it was left or was dragged out, I'm not sure. That's when I heard the voice for the first time. You know how when you think you hear your own voice. It was like that, but happened when I was already having internal dialogue, I can't exactly describe it, but it sounded a little off. It told me to go back home. That was the big paranormal event, while in high school I was clapping my girl's cheeks, and after she fell asleep on my chest. I laid back on my pillow, grabbed her booty with my right hand, kissed her on her head, and followed suit. We were woken by my Jack Russell terrier growling at the stairs from her dog bed. It sounded like someone was jogging up them. I thought it was my dad, so I covered up my girl and wrapped myself in a towel to check it out. I checked the whole house, and nobody was there except my girl and me. All the doors were locked. Back to 2021, I was back on the rez and the Latina women from town loved me. I had a co-worker come over. She wanted to date so I told her the rules. She said she was a virgin, which was not true, I called bullshit, and she blushed. She was very inexperienced but not a virgin and, more importantly, seemed like an awesome girl, so I told her if you bring me peace, I'll take care of you. When we first hung out the sky went crazy. It was a clear day but out of nowhere, with no warning, lightning was everywhere. Padme told me she said ('Sorry spirits'). She was amazing and would do all kinds of things, her family also treated me great. It was a 180-degree turn compared to being called a tree nigger like I had been in the past lol. I hate that word, but I got to use it for the story so it's the whole truth.

One weekend we went to the beach and stayed at a well-known, particularly beautiful hotel and had a great time. We'll call the hotel Inn on the Beach. This beautiful brunette knocked on the door and asked me if she could come inside with puppy eyes. Lmfao this was a first for me and I was excited two at the same time! I didn't want to disrespect Padme, so I declined her. Later in the year, I was going to my dad's land assignment to shoot my Glock 34, and she asked to come. She wasn't a bad shot, just not a great one. However, she said something foreboding ('this would be a good place for houses'). Damn, my family must be a joke to her clan I thought. She was from the same reservation. Her dad's clan is huge and one of the most powerful on the reservation. Mine is the smallest clan on the Reservation. Before getting together, we made sure we weren't even remotely related. I had a strict schedule work, Jiu-jitsu, running, and lifting. After a year of dating, she was still a great woman to me, so I figured I'd introduce her to my family then get serious about getting a better job.

I hung out with my brother, and we had a great time. My mom who I trusted lied and told my girl she shouldn't be with me because I'm indecisive. I am many things, but not indecisive. Looking back, she was co-dependent and didn't want me to have my own life. It would threaten her control over me. I didn't find out about that until a year later. This didn't ruin our friendship; she is still my mom, and we talked it out. She has more respect for me now and we get along great. When I got back to the rez, I joined the military to get a better job when I returned home. I was a reservist. It seemed like a great plan to be back in one year and I'd grab my girl a ring since she loved those. Women who are not sluts or backstabbers have abilities men don't have; they can feel things in the spiritual realm. ('See you soon babe') I said to my girl who had wet eyes and didn't want me to go, I believe it was her spiritual insight.

I knew I'd be successful, and nothing would stop me unless I physically could not continue. She wrote to me the whole time I was gone. Lmfao I won't bullshit you, if I didn't think I had a future family back home I would not have endured that. I would rather box and roll on the mats than that any day of the week. Critically though I did believe that, so mentally I was unstoppable.

I got fucked with a lot in training, almost entirely due to my own shortcomings. I was terrible at marching at first. I spent many nights scuzzing the floor, doing pull-ups, or holding something out while squatting against a wall until the lactic acid would no longer allow me to do so. The most hilarious thing I had to do was yell the words "suicidal thoughts" for three hours at the top of my lungs lol. That shit sounds retarded but was hilarious in real life.

My girl's letters were amazing ('To my handsome, I think about you all day. I can't wait to be in your arms again. My sister said she likes you because she knows how happy you make me.') I left it on top of my bag and someone else read it too because it was on the bottom of the bag when I woke up, someone put it under all my clothes. The DI had me outside getting that IT in bright and early lol. I fucking did it too, I came home and my girl and I were happy.

CHAPTER 2

I come from a terrible family. My Aunt Jolly is a well-known witch and has murdered a man. She lit his house on fire right next to the water heater, so it looked like a mistake. He was in the shower, and they had an intense argument that day. Her daughter is also a witch she uses Ouija boards and casts spells, all that rotten stuff. However, I feel sympathy for her mom Jolly, from what I know she was a flirty teen and was raped. I believe this because at least one of the women I have loved was raped. It fucks people up bad. I imagine that is a big factor in why she is evil today. I also believe that's why old Indians would skin rapists alive, it's just as bad as being a murderer.

 I had three uncles. Two were good people who had terrible things happen to them and essentially became drunks. One is completely consumed by greed, akin to dragon sickness from the LOTR universe. He made thousands of dollars selling drugs and killing his own community. His name is Bu, and he is slick, very socially intelligent and disciplined. Most people who have met him likely have no idea who is in front of them. They see a seemingly inspirational rancher and businessman of impeccable integrity and commitment. Although some of these things are true, inside that man also lay a murderous rage and insatiable greed. Even I would probably not know this had I not been in his family and the son of his brother. My father still bears the scars from when Bu tried to blind him in one eye with a Red Ryder BB gun. He still remembers when a fist fight Bu lost turned into an attempt to murder my dad with a car jack. After this, Dad spent two weeks working in the mountains.

My dad was a contractor working with the forest service at the time. Chunk, my uncle, found Bu waiting for my dad to return home holding a Ruger mini-14, which is a .556 M14. Chunk took it from him and likely saved my dad's life in the process. While we lived in Oregon my aunt mailed my father an undisclosed to me book and a movie called *The Bone Collector*. The letter accompanying these items was meant to convince my dad to murder a man named Son who lived north of his land assignment. As I write this Jolly, my dad's sister, has said two things to me ('I'm gonna burn your fucking house down!') with everyone in it, as well as ('Hi G'). I was dating a woman from an enormous well-respected clan. So, it felt good to do something honorable to make it clear I was not like my aunt. Especially because Padme's Grandpa didn't approve of me due to my family. ('Do you know who his grandmother is?') he asked Padme. My family is known to be no good. I can't blame him for thinking like that.

The base I was on had mandatory HBL, holiday block leave. Which meant I'd be home for Christmas. When I got home everything was awesome, she picked me up at the airport and things were great. Two things sealed my fate and taught me a valuable lesson, but it was a motherfucker to go through. Padme's Aunt Dani told her after we had been together for two years that we were cousins, and I got physically sick, throwing up all of that. The worst part was her tears just running down her face. She kept asking me ('Why would God do this to us G?!') The sky did that thing again, it went from clear to lightning in an odd fast way, like a light switch. I didn't have an answer for her at the time. I wasn't doing anything fucked up so the Creator would not just punish me for fun. I was very fucking mad, like I have never been before, we checked this before we did anything.

I knew I could make this right by proving it was a lie, but I underestimated the power of the tongue and metaphorically shot myself in the foot. I told her ('babe, you passed all my tests. I expected you to cheat while I was in the core, but you didn't. When I get home we can get a blood test to prove it's a lie.') I was a shameful sight to behold at LAX, buzzcut and still throwing up, hopelessly depressed. I had money so I figured I'd get drunk. It had been two years since I got drunk, and it seemed like a terrible time to do so but I wanted to. Since my military scheduled flight left thirty minutes early, I had to reschedule. This gave me an hour to burn. The woman behind the desk made my life easy, she kicked ass at her job. I had a conversation with a rich gay man at the bar. I usually don't hang out with homosexuals, not because I hate them, it just makes me feel uneasy being around a dude who likes dudes. I also hate television for pushing homosexual agendas on my people while at the same time encouraging our women to be sluts so they can run through them.

Padme told her friends what her aunt told her. She said she still loved me and wanted to stay with me if it was a lie. However, her friends told her to fuck another dude, and if she still wanted me after it was meant to be. Terrible advice, of course, but one of them is a single mom and the other is a club slut, so no surprises there. Since I opened my mouth and said I expected her to cheat when she didn't, I spoke it into reality and Padme fucked the EMT while I was back on base. While on base I told my girl I'd like to be transferred to a base farther north to be around my dad, he was only expected to live a certain number of years although I know he will prove them wrong. When I got home, I kept hearing this voice telling me ('isn't this what you asked for? We are helping you.') I had a conversation with these people I said ('NO! I wanted to see my dad for a couple of weeks in case he dies, not lose my fiancé and live with this shame!') This happened on my dad's land on the reservation. While driving I heard the voice again ('We are helping you, don't you remember she had that dream about you leaving the reservation.') Me ('who the fuck is speaking to me?! You slippery sons of bitches. If I find out who you are I'm going to cut the skin between your Achilles tendon and ankle. Run a rope between it, hoist you up an oak tree and skin you alive when I find out who you are.') I know that's not grammatically correct but that's exactly how it was spoken.

Me to myself out loud in my car I trusted these motherfuckers. I forgave them for sterilizing native women until the late 1970s and they dare to use this weapon against me?... it might not be the US government though I can't overreact. I wasn't sure if that was God or man but logic told me it was manmade, why else would they say we? I was boiling with rage it, felt like God stabbed me in the back... still depressed from how miserable this had made my fiancé. A few months later, in spring, I was angry and told God what I thought without holding back. You told me to come home. I stopped dealing and came home then got an honest job. You rewarded me by stabbing me in the fucking back! This book is a crock of shit, so much for never forsaking the righteous. I followed your rules I didn't eat pork or shrimp; you did this to me for fun fuck you.

After all this, I did something that brought me misery and taught me a lesson on remaining in my place. I got a Tarot Card reading to understand the situation better. I meant to solve the issue and help my girl and me. It was terrifyingly accurate and unforgivably stupid of me. She fanned out the cards. And told me to move my hand over them picking the one that feels hot. I assumed I had wasted my money, and this was a gimmick. I was wrong. I felt a card that emitted heat near the right side of the fanned-out deck. I touched it and she set it up. We continued until I didn't feel the heat anymore. She then told me what they said. She said there was some horrible lie told to cause a separation and there would be a reunion. She was extremely specific, she said it was an aunt, lastly this is the beginning of a new time, and I can either let life happen to me or make it happen. Unfortunately, that seemed to come true. I hooked up with an awesome chick from the desert she wanted me to meet her parents, and I should have but didn't. After the reading things got worse, Padme looked different, her eyes looked different. I decided to ask the creator if the voice was not his.

SECOND HALF-ACCEPTANCE

I asked for a ridiculous event. If those voices were not you, make it impossible for me to go to drill this weekend. Make it huge and extremely obvious I don't know what the fuck is going on. I'm hopelessly confused and if I don't know you exist, I'm not living by any rules anymore the world is a savage place. I went to bed thinking this was the beginning of me living without rules and winning by any means necessary. I woke and got ready to leave only to find that the river was splashing over the bridge connecting the ranch to the road. Across the bridge the road was washed out completely. This overwhelmed me and I had no choice but to accept what it meant. When I went to drill the Officers and high ranking enlisted looked at me like I was A Martian. It was like they knew I spoke back those months ago and like they knew what just happened. It sickened me to think that was true but, that's what happened. I tried to ignore the coincidence but could not forget it. I eventually decided if they were willing to do this to me and possibly to other citizens, I would no longer serve that establishment. I showed up for the late September drill and never came back. I decided if that's how evil they are I would be breaking my oath to continue to serve. "I (STATE YOUR NAME) DO SOLEMNLY SWEAR (OR AFFIRM) THAT I WILL SUPPORT AND DEFEND THE CONSTITUTION OF THE UNITED STATES AGAINST ALL ENEMIES, FOREIGN AND DOMESTIC; THAT I WILL BEAR TRUE FAITH AND ALLEGIANCE TO THE SAME; AND THAT I WILL OBEY THE ORDERS OF THE PRESIDENT OF THE UNITED STATES AND THE ORDERS OF THE OFFICERS ... " This is a direct violation of the rights of citizens of the United States and a Violation of the Treaty they made with my Tribe. I hated them for it, this incident pushed me into an extreme state of depression and rage, even though I wish I could deny what happened to me I lived through it and I'm completely coherent it did happen. I can't change that, and I won't forget it because it was something my mind won't forget.

It never happened again but if I tell anyone a doctor or such. They could label me crazy and give me drugs which I don't want. This scenario took my ability to get intoxicated at all. Now I just remember what happened and must be sober because while intoxicated I feel too sad. I must have revenge I can never forgive them for what they did to her. Her tears, her pain I will make them suffer for all of it. I remember her smiling and how happy she was with me. She claimed she was raped by her dad. ('I had to be waiting in the bathroom when he got home.') He seemed like a good person, but she did have daddy issues no telling what's true for sure. I hate how perfect their plan was. My girl had memory issues due to brain surgery. I'll look crazy if I tell the truth. Over time, she may not even remember all the details. It makes sense though I do too much research and if we were married it would make the reservation much more difficult for an outsider to influence. I will repay the NSA for what they did, when possible. They have committed a war crime against my nation and tormented me and my fiancé.

Ade Padme's mom, asked me the first time she met me what I thought of Jolly. I should have pieced it together, but I never did. Ade and Dar are best friends and used to play with a Ouija board together. It all makes sense now Padme was an innocent victim of an elaborate plot. They thought the shame of believing I was with my cousin would make me leave the reservation. Since Ray allegedly used to raped Padme regularly and Padme told me she told her mom more than once. Her mom Ade controls the family completely. Ray can't do the right thing because his wife could ruin him with that information. Which makes Dar almost untouchable. My dad is only here for one season of the year. Jolly, Bu, and Dar went to the council and took my dad's land assignment. A year before this Gram gave 13.2 acres to my dad and had it notarized. Ray Padme's stepdad has a powerful family member named Eil a close friend of Bu's. He wanted to go down to the care home to make my gram sign a new document and notarize it. These were the worst days of my life.

For six months my family and I were harassed by the Tribal Police at least once a week. Dar would call the cops for my sister's horse making noise, leave grams front gate open. Which gram never did. Jolly said ('Freyja is just moving home to die.') Kelly the caretaker called my dad over and she said Jolly and Dar were roughing Freyja up. Trying to get her to sigh a new will. She had bruises all over her apparently it was caused by high blood pressure. This pissed me off that bitch Dar can get away with anything because her best friend is married to the chief of police.

The Tribe gave my dad his land finally, so we began building a fence. Jolly called the cops again. A young fat cop showed up a Mexican guy from town. He shook my hand, his whole body shaking and said he heard there was an unauthorized fence being built. I let my dad do the talking and we stopped. Dad told me to be careful Jolly would love for me to get killed by police. Which statistically is likely I'm 6'2, 200 pounds ,9 percent body fat and a native male. I did, however, ask the cop if they found out who put the bruises on my gram. He nervously said it was determined to be high blood pressure.

My dad called the police station and said we had papers to prove it was ours. For proper understanding understand we natives did everything verbal without paper, so most families don't have deeds. We never needed them until our government became corrupt. Dad said Dar was in conflict because she is best friends with Ade. I suggested he say it. Since then, TPD has not been back for 3 months. The most disgusting part of all this is Padme is not related to me. The last time I saw her Dar stopped on the road and tried to talk to me. I drove past by that point I had learned my lesson about speaking to a witch. I understand why she wanted to talk though. Dar really did date her cousin for about a year. She knew how I felt it was likely planned out. She had no idea he was related to her because her mom never told her.

Bu was using a three-signature loophole to take my dad's land. The purpose of that law was so the people could object and remove a law the Tribal council passed. Not to draw time so you can make my gram sigh a will Bu and Jolly made. That's not the intent of the law. Which is likely why Char didn't show up to either council meeting I went to. She has a degree in law and surely understands this. There is a chance she was just sick though she seems like a very good person. Padme if this ever hits your ears I forgive you. I don't hold a grudge against you for fucking the EMT while I was in the core. I'm sorry I brought that evil around you when I got a reading by the cards. I saw how it changed you. Your eyes your voice I wish you the best but can't tolerate disrespect it sets a bad example for the young brothers.

Her workplace had cabinets opening and closing. Last I saw she had chosen the streets unfortunately. Bu wants my dad's piece of land because he wants to put a bridge across the river. This is to make money off selling the family ranch to the tribe which is illegal. He would just get them to pay him well to make the roads and house pads. When everything was over, we finally got it in writing. My sister's appendix almost burst she made it to the hospital in time. They removed it. I can't prove it, but I suspect foul play Jolly is next door with gram. My sister now has spots on her liver. The doctor didn't know what it was but I think that's strange because she never drinks alcohol. They will live to regret this. I want to torture the NSA, not my fellow tribal members. They simply don't understand the reality of our situation but if I torture the NSA, it will shame the core, so I won't do any of that I'll expose them.

When the day comes that the NSA and CIA are proven to be as evil as I know they are. They will be destroyed by the people.

***

My dad and I were able to have three beers each and enjoy hanging out around the fire. So, it's getting better. It is a very hopeless feeling to know the government has this kind of weapon. Yet we Natives still have the same government that was designed to fail given to us by the BIA. The mission statement for the BIA was that once all the Tribes had proper functional governments, they would disband it. Effectively if you do your job right you work yourself out of a job. I began my research could the United States still be waging war against us covertly. COINTELPRO was a CIA project designed to infiltrate all groups and communities in the United States down to the Tribal ones… MK ULTRA was a loosely observed project to attempt to find a way to get a human being to commit an assassination on word. They laced innocent white American citizens with LSD to get someone to confess to anything. The CIA murdered a man by throwing him out a window of a high raise. George White A CIA agent working in operation midnight climax is quoted as saying this in a letter to a colleague. ('of course I was a very minor missionary actually a heretic, but I toiled wholeheartedly in the vineyards because it was fun, fun, fun. Where else could a red-blooded American boy Lie, kill and cheat, steal, deceive, rape and pillage with the sanction and blessing of the all-highest?')

The CIA did this to white people and until 1979 California still had eugenics laws in place my mother and my father were born before the law was removed. White and black even some redskins if they are in Law Enforcement are working for these godless savages. The government lies to our native women telling them they are equal to men. They encourage them with TV and music to be sluts. Most of them will have fucked five men by the time they get out of high school losing their ability to pair bond correctly. Which means they will likely become single mothers. By being so increasing the chance of their children being enslaved in the corporate prison or plantation system by twenty times. The government uses rap music to encourage our young brothers to kill each other and use their women just for sex. While also encouraging them to drink and use drugs. All this works against my nation because the men end up dead, on drugs, or in prison as slaves. Our women end up losing their ability to pair bond correctly. Which makes them easy to fuck but not wife material.

Outside men Mexicans, whites, blacks. Knock our women up and end up living on the reservation. Other men's children are inheriting our tribal land. While our men who are from here and are truly native. End up not producing kids and are either dead, on drugs, or enslaved. America is killing my tribe. The education system is set up for women. Intended to get them ran through in college. Three companies (Warner Records, Universal music group, and Sony music group) control around 90 percent of the depiction of hip hop. Core civic (Formerly CCA Corrections Corporation of America.) and Geo group own almost all private prison beds in the USA. Connected by vanguard and black rock which are the largest shareholders in both media and prisons. Therapists don't teach to improve communities or help anyone they are adversaries of us. Minorites more so but even the lower-class white men and their beautiful communities. A therapist's job is to make all their patient's better members of the Government. They have been trained to do this. Split up families just like CPS split us up so they can destroy us.

Sex traffic our women whatever they want. We as Native American people must prioritize giving land assignments to our young native men. The government is systematically killing us. Single mothers should not be allowed land assignments. I don't care how much hate I get for this the future of my collective race is at hand. If your feelings are more important than my entire race fuck you. In nature women are always born in higher number than men. If the United States controls our women, they control our NATION. They can breed us out and kill our men. We should not follow their laws that disarm us, we should have modern guns. Our own Militia. Like a forjd with a small full time professional military. The government still castrates us like they used to. They encourage our men to be gay or trans. California just passed a law to allow children to do this easier. These disgusting motherfuckers used our respect of women against us.

CHAPTER 3- UNDERSTANDING OUR ENEMY AND HOW TO COMBAT THEM

The founding fathers of America are freemasons, this is common knowledge today. However, I bet you are not aware freemasons used to be called stonemasons. An ancient satanic cult who killed King Soloman. The United States has always been a satanic nation. The leadership is evil, all of them. Twitler chose Andrew Jackson as his oval office statue. Mr. Ban is known to be a high ranking white supremist. Recently they tried to ban the bible. The reason is in Revelations 2:9 KJV ('I know thy works, and tribulations, and poverty') ('but thou art rich') ('and I know the blasphemy of them which say they are Jews, and are not, but are the synagogue of Satan') the biblical Jews are the black people who live around the Mississippi river. Read Deuteronomy chapter 28 this is very specific and could only mean one people. Deuteronomy 28:22 22 The LORD shall smite thee with a consumption, and with a fever, and with an inflammation, and with an extreme burning, and with the sword, and with blasting, and with mildew; and they shall pursue thee until thou perish.

Smallpox caused fever and aching pain as well as rashes then scabs. It could even leave you blind, which is a curse in the chapter listed. Extreme burning could be seen as drought from global warming. The sword is obvious and with blasting that sounds like firearms to me. Remember this book was supposedly written in the 7th century BC. Mildew could be strange funguses the Europeans brought here that killed lots of trees. It could also be talking about how smallpox looks like a carpet filled with black mold. The last part is clear. I believe this verse is for us Natives not blacks because they didn't die to disease like we did. Read the entire chapter it could be that this is for us, and the others are what he is saying to the black people. He might not differentiate between his people.

Genesis 15:13-14 KJV

[13] And he said unto Abram, know of a surety that thy seed shall be a stranger in a land that is not theirs, and shall serve them; and they shall afflict them four hundred years.

[14] And also that nation, whom they shall serve, will I judge: and afterward shall they come out with great substance.

The Almighty sent these nations against his people to punish them for not obeying him. In hopes they would be jealous and want their position back as his people. He sees how the colonizers are killing his people, and he is going to judge them for their crimes. My Tribe has nine tribal council members. Gad is the Ninth Tribe of Israel. The Navajo have an origin story that started with a flood. The story is almost the exact same one, it even has Noah in it and possibly his real name.

Waynaboozhoo and the Great Flood
an Ojibwe legend
retold by Valerie Connors

Long ago the world was filled with evil. Men and women lost respect for each other. The Creator was unhappy about this and decided to cause a great flood to purify the earth.

A man named Waynaboozhoo survived. He turned some floating sticks and a log into a raft for the animals and himself. They floated around for a full moon waiting for the water to go down. It didn't, so Waynaboozhoo decided to do something about it.

"Maang!" he called to the loon. "You are an excellent swimmer. See if you can dive down to the Old World and bring back a lump of mud in your bill. With mud, I will create a New World."

Maang dove into the water and was gone a long time. When he finally did return, he said, "I could not reach the Old World. It was too far down."

"Amik!" called Waynaboozhoo to the beaver. "You are an excellent swimmer. Will you try next?"

Amik dove off and was gone even longer than Maang, but he too returned empty-handed.

"Is there anyone else who'll try?" asked Waynaboozhoo.

Just then a small coot, Aajigade, came swimming along and asked, "What's going on?"

"Get away Aajigade," called one of the birds. "We do not have time for your nonsense."

Now the animals began arguing loudly. Everyone had a different plan about how to get the mud, but no one could agree on whose plan they would use. For hours and hours they argued. By and by, someone noticed that the sun was beginning to go down. They would have to put off the planning until the next day. Everyone began to find his or her sleeping spot on the raft to rest for the night. Maang asked, "Whatever happened to that silly little Aajigade?"

Suddenly, there was shouting on the other end of the raft. Someone had noticed a small body floating in the water. Water birds paddled hurriedly to investigate and found that it was Aajigade. They brought his body to the raft.

Waynaboozhoo lifted him up, and looking in his small beak, he found a particle of mud. Little Aajigade had reached the Old World and got the mud! He had given his life to do this. The other animals were ashamed of themselves for having made fun of little Aajigade. They hung their heads. They felt very sad.

Waynaboozhoo took Aajigade's little body and softly blew life back into him. Waynaboozhoo held him closely to warm him and announced that from that day forward, Aajigade would always retain a place of honor among the animals.

Waynaboozhoo set Aajigade down on the water and he swam off as though nothing had happened.

Then Waynaboozhoo took Aajigade's mud in his hands and began to shape it. Next he commanded it to grow. As it grew, he needed a place to put it. Mikinaak (the snapping turtle) came forward and said, "I have a broad back. Place it here."

Waynaboozhoo put it on Mikinaak's back so that it could grow larger.

"Miigwetch, Mikinaak," said Waynaboozhoo. "From this day on, you shall have the ability to live in all the worlds, under the mud, in the water, and on land."

The mud began to take the shape of land. Waynaboozhoo placed some tiny enigoonsags (ants) on it. This made it start to spin and grow more. It grew and grew, and more animals stepped onto it until finally it was large enough for moose to walk about. Now Waynaboozhoo sent benishiyag (the birds) to fly around to survey how large the land was. He said to them, "Return to me now and again to let me know how the land is doing. Send back your messages with songs. To this day, that is what the birds continue to do. That is also why they are called the singers.

At last, Waynaboozhoo stepped onto the New World. It had become a home, a place for all the animals, insects and birds, a place for all living things to live in harmony.

***

Many skins including I were taught not to hold hate. Not to focus on or be afraid of an evil spirit if it's around. They can feed on your fear. That is Old Testament knowledge how did our ancestors know this then? The government told us in school we come from Asia. Explain to me then how pure Native Americans don't have any Neanderthal or Denisovan DNA. That doesn't make sense because all homo-sapiens from Europe and Asia. Have a small amount of DNA from one of these two groups.

Margaret Sanger said in 1939 ('We do not want word to go out that we want to exterminate the Negro population.') 61,051,230 estimated abortions have been performed since 1973-2023. 39.2 percent of those were done to non-Hispanic blacks this is genocide. It's sickening how well thought out the plan truly is. They get to enslave the men and systematically exterminate the Hebrews. While seemingly giving women rights to save face. For extra fun they divided the families so it's easy to sex traffic our women. Native women and black women are the most missing annually per capita. It's not even close. Native women are twelve times more likely to go missing than any other demographic. They showcase our women with Awareness Day for missing or murdered indigenous women and girls. This satanic kingdom has polluted our minds with porn turned our women against us. Made us see them as objects instead of our star player. We as men are the coach and women are the star players in our nation. Raising our babies bringing us peace. There is not an indigenous men's day. However, we as Native men are the most likely per capita to be murdered by police. This nation has had the Patriot Act in place since October 26, 2001, and now has the USA FREEDOM ACT. So, since 2001 America has been a police state. You expect me to believe that those missing people can't be found? In a Nation where the government legally listens to you through your phone? They can watch you fuck your girlfriend or boyfriend from the tv facing your bed, if the footage doesn't serve them, they delete it. If they can be trusted to do so that, is we don't really know for sure. Everyone carries phones around. I don't believe they can't find these missing people it seems foolish. I believe they allow it and participate in it.

JFK warned his nation about these people and the CIA killed him. From 1973-1976 3,406 Native women were sterilized. Bush served as the DCI for 355 days from January 30, 1976, to January 20, 1977. His son who was president from 2001 to 2009 passed the Patriot Act. The CIA has violated the Constitution of the United States of America. They have done so by bypassing the checks and balances, threw creating an American police state. Seizing control of our nation and changing it from a representative republic to an Autocratic Empire. In doing so they have crippled the nation by dividing the people. Who rightfully don't trust the government anymore.

Today we have the far left who are essentially communists. They claim to support us minorities but support the weapons of our extermination, abortion and the feminism movement. As well as homosexuality being pushed on our young men, encouraging our little boys to have their genitals cut off. Sounds a lot like how they used to use our ball sacks to hold tobacco in the 1800s. You brainwash our innocent daughters ruin their ability to pair bond correctly! Steal them for your personal toys, use them to raise colonizer's children on our reservations or raise native boys to be enslaved. While my brothers work on your plantations making 13 cents an hour! While in prison you buck break our brothers. Expose them to drugs and experiment on them. You have tormented me with your insidious weapon. Taken my woman, my dignity. Mercilessly inflicted pain on her and successfully implemented a system. To eradicate my nation. I have a scripture for you sons of bitches.

Ezekiel 25:17 KJV

('And I will execute great vengeance upon them with furious rebukes; and they shall know that I am the lord, when I shall lay my vengeance upon them.') Mr. Newsom whatever puppet stands as president next. Let my people go. This is my call to all my brothers willing to fight. Prepare form militia's stock ammunition and knowledge. Educate the youth of our enemy and their weapons being used against us. Do not underestimate the enemy and remember Ephesians 6:12 KJV, Isaiah 54:17 KJV. Don't do drugs I've done LSD three times, mushrooms three times and luckily was in a white area of America. Almost nobody ever got bad drugs there but at home. You can't even trust the weed.

Lots of us get hurt or die from bad drugs. My Tribe has a jail but no clean water, our elders die from cancer at a rate you don't see in any white community. What does that tell you? We must remove the government given to us by the BIA. They purposely set it up to fail. Our Tribal governments need to be held accountable and our natural order of man leading must be restored. We should do away with Tribal Police and just have a small full-time professional force. Reenforced by everyman and potentially his wife as well, being equip with a modern rifle. I recommend an AK-74 for its reliability and lack of recoil. This rifle is easy to use and with an optic very versatile. It is worth looking into a battle rifle cambered in a bigger caliber for potentially dealing with armor. Training can of course help deal with armored enemies. It's a good idea to be able to produce our own ammunition.

As of now the feds own our ground and we have no rights to the water running through our nation. Recently the world watched as the IDF bombed hospitals marched into a city and disarmed its civilian population. Then proceeded to starve and kill them. Make no mistake the United States is the exact same nation it was in 1776. They didn't simply revolt because of the king's tax rate. The English crown prevented Anglo- American colonists from moving west. Of the Appalachian Mountain range because of the Royal Proclamation of 1763. Which was a result of Indian Nations carrying an English victory over the French. In the French and Indian wars. The government has in place as I write discriminating laws against minorities as a psychological weapon. It is easier for a Native man or Black man to get into college than a white man. This is not to help us but a sophisticated mechanism to subconsciously tell you that you are not equal to whites.

The United States hates us we must help our brothers from impoverished tribes. Then seek to help our brothers with hair like wool along the Mississippi. After of course we are in good unity and our nations are in good standing. US law enforcement or slave catchers should not be allowed in our nations at all. If I had it my way, they would be shot on sight for entering the reservation. It's a national security risk, they are never here to do anything good and don't belong here. Tribal police should not exist because one clan will always have too much power if they do. I am completely aware this story could get me in serious shit. The power structure won't like it. I made a promise to the god of Abraham, Issac and Jacob if he kept my family safe through this hell. I would record my story and tell his people. Nothing instills more fear in me than betraying him.

To the white folks who are good people. If I was Chinese, I would infiltrate your nation exploiting. Your violations of the Constitution of the United States of America to. Create a closet communist party with intentions to further divide your great nation. Once the population is ripe for insurrection I'd back the puppet communist state. This is the only way I could conquer you, without being turned to glass from your atomic weapons. I'd prefer to have my puppet state along your west coast with Cali, Oregon, Washington. This would suit my plan because I could support these states from the Pacific Ocean. Possibly soldiers come in mass numbers through loose immigration laws. The best-case scenario is to simply offer your citizens whose rights have been violated. Assistance in creating their own communist nation. Perhaps even get most of your politicians to be communists. Or right-wing fascists in support of a feudalistic system.

In this system the police would have access to weapons that civilians could not own. They could have a separate set of rights that protects them. We'll call it selective immunity, and they would not be held accountable for their actions. Treasonous or otherwise. They would serve the king and be first class citizens above the common peasant. Skin color wouldn't matter if they do as they are told. You could use them to disarm the civilian population by convincing the mothers of America. School is safer with more gun bans. Neglecting to remember your old weapon that smashed. Your past enemies which were having a heavily armed civilian population. That was extremely effective because if everyone shot it's possible to raise an enormous army. In a very short time who will outshoot the enemy. Because they shot more. Like a boxer who trained his whole life vs a boxer who trained for six months. The best thing you could do to stop your enemy is simply follow your ancestor's constitution and not let any state infringe on it.

However, if you want to make your enemies' job easy. You could keep infringing on your citizen's rights. Further isolating them against you. Keep waging a war against the minority populations in your nation. Well, saving face and disguising it as helping them. Perhaps even continue colonizing the world through a puppet state. While your economy can no longer fund it. California just two years ago passed a bill to pay. Those who were sterilized in the 20th century. Until 1979 it still had its eugenics laws in place. The mass sterilization was roughly 60,000. My cousin was recently on the Tribal council and received a letter from Mr. Newsom. The message was essentially we are sorry for going from paying 5 dollars per severed head. To gently trying to exterminate you through eugenics, openly sterilizing your women until the late 1970s. Now we would like to be friends. He left out the part where he stated what the new intention is.

Good morning Dumbfucks! I would like to leave a physical trail of evidence I support you. The reason I want to do so is. We currently have a plan in place to destroy you in approximately 100-200 years at maximum. Here is how we will do it! First, we will get you to trust us. We'll help you attend college and pretend we care about your women. The education system is designed for women. This serves two purposes. To keep your men from becoming educated. As well as keep your women with the desire to go to college. We can get your women more loyal to the United States Government. Who used to rape and or kill you, murder, enslave, sometimes castrate your family members dads, brothers. Usually, we murdered them as well. Now of course we told you that in school we are just not as brutally honest as the author is. In a sneaky way we told you though. Although what we absolutely could not tell you is.

While we were still openly attempting to kill you all. We received backlash from the mothers of our soldiers who were killed by your nation's soldiers. Disease made it easy enough to kill most of you. Unfortunately, some of you are extremely capable and we could not kill you all. Have no fear modern genocide is here! We will destroy your family structure to weaken the nations. Then we will enslave your men, this will be easy we designed school for them to not be interested. Then we will use rap to encourage them to kill each other. Use TV, cartoons with mice read between the lines. Founded by an open satanist, to encourage your men to be gay. Use video games its ok to have a big Hawaiian man in it but he must be gay. The straight ones will be pushed to pump and dump women. While avoiding having kids at all costs. Hashtag fuck them kids. We will tell your women its ok to murder their unborn babies it's easy and completely confidential. We will teach them being a whore is more fun than being a mother.

That they can sleep with as many men as they wish. In their ignorance they will easily sleep with more than five. After five they won't produce the same amount of a neuro chemical needed to pair bond. Obviously sabotaging their natural ability to be mothers and keepers of home. This is great for us! We get to fuck your women send them back home ran through. Setting them up to become single mothers being twenty times more likely to raise children who will be incarcerated or enslaved. Don't worry that's just what happens to your young native males. The single mothers who don't understand the whole picture. Truly believe it is men to blame instead of who did it. The United States Government. The process continues with the next generation but this time it's easier because we have our weapons already listed. As well as the bitter single mom who at heart is COMPLETELY INNOCENT, she was just brainwashed since she was a little girl by the system. We only care about her while she is young it was her god given right to grow old with her husband who she got with as a young woman. She was supposed to be able to watch her family and nation grow and prosper. Now she gets to live the second half of her life alone, watching her nation be exterminated. Until we have conquered you it's just like before but this time we can save face globally. Hell history will remember it as the government helping women the irony of that!

Have you asked yourself why they want to control all the communities in America down to the tribal ones? What is their goal? Protect us from some enemy across the ocean as they always say. More likely it's the same intentions Benjamin Franklin had. In his autobiography ('And indeed if it be the design of providence to extirpate these savages in order to make room for cultivators of the earth, it seems not improbable that rum may be the appointed means.') The intention is to destroy us and the blacks. In 1998 B. Franklin's house was renovated. Ten individual's remains were found. Six of them Identified as children. Mr. Franklin was one of America's most noticeable Freemasons. He served the devil most people in America are atheist. The ones who control it are devoted servants of evil spirits and behave as such.

I recommend you native men have as many kids as possible and at least one son to pass your land to. It is almost hopeless our women have been brainwashed. We must be as ruthless as the enemy we face. Above all we need to control our nations, as well as stop internal conflict. Respect your brother, you have a common enemy. My family still has an old 45-70 taken off the enemy's corpse when he collapsed off his standard issue horse. It's still war just with modern technology. The meaning of those dreams was the most high telling me I would become a marine I would do something that cost me my beloved wife. After that I could wallow in my misery and hatred knowing it's possible the government sent me all the dreams and sent her the one, she had. Or I could accept what I have done regardless of their deeds and the Voice to Skull weapon. Tell the world about it and help god's people wake up and fight back. Regardless of what comes from telling the truth. The creator destroyed the world with a flood and says he will use fire next. Have as many sons and daughters as possible and be ready. Make your circle of survivors for when the time comes.

As for the Delilah spirit that has tormented my family for four generations. I banish you from my family and my Tribe. You were attached to my family first and now you are running around my community. You better leave before I die because if you don't, I'm going to slice you into pieces and drag you back myself bitch. I am still a logic-based man my great grandfather Fred was abducted by aliens everyone's heard the story on the res. I wonder if the aliens wanted to look at him because he was a full-blooded man from the tribe of Gad. We as humans can control the weather like in Dubai who says aliens could not do the same. Hypothetically if Aliens wanted to why couldn't they split a sea. Currently Jolly called the TPD to try to get the lower part of my dad's land again, that's where they intend to build the road and bridge to cross the river. Remember brothers love our women it is not their fault things are the way they are. They are helpless puppies being abused and brainwashed by a Satanic system. We should marry our women off to other tribes to maximize our population and future prosperity.

I hated that book so much I miss being stupid not knowing how things really are. I miss being happy. I will say that without it I would have shot myself when the voice to skull weapon was used against me so I'm thankful. My hatred of them and desire to help my people and all innocent subjects of the USA, has kept me alive all this time. I do not care about your politics. I do not care about your fake republic. I only live to see you die.

Akin to Grievous I know live in constant misery and often wish I never survived. I couldn't save her, and everything continues my people draw closer to extermination with every passing generation. Look up Street Cops and listen to the fat guy talk about how good sex feels after killing someone. Listen to the ex-special forces guy teach cops to treat citizens like Arab insurgents. If there is a civil war I will have my revenge. This is a fictional story.

www.ingramcontent.com/pod-product-compliance
Lightning Source LLC
LaVergne TN
LVHW092101060526
838201LV00047B/1513